# Simon the Snake

By Diane Blue Brooks Britt

Illustrated by Alyssa Grizenko

Simon the Snake
Illustrator: Alyssa Grizenko

Intended for ages 0 and up



Publisher: Caterpillar Books, an Imprint of Monarch Educational Services, LLC



www.monarcheducationalservices.com

First Edition

In Memory of Veirl Brooks, my
late husband, who served
as an umpire for many years.

Dedicated to my grandchildren
Henry M. Brooks and
Annabelle R. Brooks
Love,
Diane Blue Brooks Britt

Illustrator Dedication:
To my nephews and niece,
Love Aunt Alyssa

Simon the Snake lives deep in the forest where the trees are tall and shady. Below the trees, the grass is green and thick.

Simon loves crawling through the grass and listening to the birds sing, but soon Simon begins to wonder if there are any other animals he can be friends with. It isn't always fun playing by himself.

Simon thinks, I must go exploring in the forest and see if there is anyone else like me.

As Simon crawls around the forest, he sings in his squeaky, soft voice. He hopes another animal will hear him.

"Hello, my name is Simon. This is my home. I've no one to play with. I'm all alone. I'll be a good friend, you'll see. So please come out and play with me."

Soon, Simon hears a voice say, "My name is Rabbie Rabbit."

Simon looks up out of the grass and sees Rabbie the Rabbit hopping gently through the leaves. He is furry and white.

This is Simon's first friend.

Simon and Rabbie Rabbit play every day. They become the best of friends. Rabbie knows his way around the forest and all the best places to hide.

But soon, Simon and Rabbie Rabbit want other animals to play with too. So, the two of them decide to go exploring together.

Simon can barely keep up with Rabbie Rabbit because he hops so fast. Simon lies down for a rest on something soft, long, and fluffy. First, he thinks it is just a soft hill of grass and leaves.

But then ...

All of a sudden,

it begins to move!

With a voice as loud as thunder, it says,

"Who is that sitting on my tail?"

“My name is Simon Snake, and this is Rabbie Rabbit. We are looking for some friends to play with.

Who are you?" asks Simon.

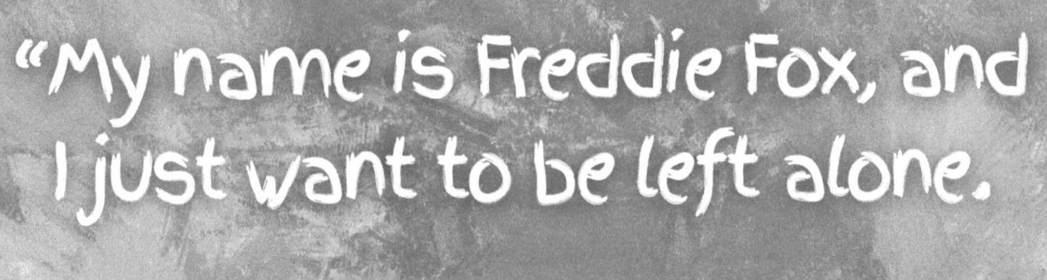

"My name is Freddie Fox, and I just want to be left alone.

I don't like being bothered. I don't like to play. I don't like talking. I just want to be alone. All by myself. Goodbye."

So. Simon and Rabbie think a minute, then share a plan. They decide to run around in a circle just to see what Freddie Fox will do.
Maybe the fox doesn't know how to play forest games or has never had an invitation.

Soon, Freddie Fox joins the circle game. Simon now knows they have another friend. Freddie does not seem grouchy anymore after that.

All three are the best of friends until they meet a bobcat named

Bobby.

With his growly voice, Bobby Bobcat says,
"Since I'm the biggest, I want to be in charge of all the games we play."
Rabbie Rabbit does not like the idea of Bobby Bobcat being in charge. Rabbie thinks all four should make decisions together because that's how friends should do things.

The first game they play is hide-and-go-seek. Freddie Fox counts to ten.

Rabbie Rabbit and Bobby Bobcat hide behind a tree.

Simon slithers down in the tall, green grass.

Simon knows he has a good chance of winning because he is the same color as the grass. Simon is the last to be found. He is the winner of hide-and-go-seek.

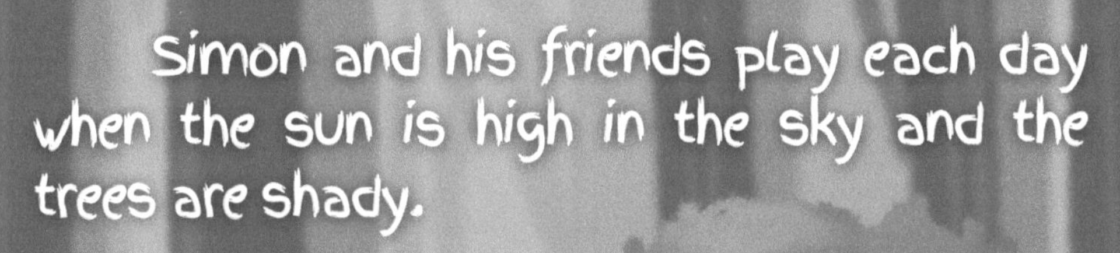

Simon and his friends play each day when the sun is high in the sky and the trees are shady.

Simon feels so happy he has made new friends, even if Bobby Bobcat wants to be bossy at times. Of all the friends Simon has, Rabbie Rabbit is his closest friend. It's probably because he met him first.

Hide-and-go-seek is a good game, but since Simon wins each time. Rabbie Rabbit has another game he wants to play that is more challenging. The game is called
baseball.
"Baseball?" asks Simon.
"I've neve
played that
game
before."

Rabbie Rabbit explains to Simon and his friends how the game is played. He tells the rules of the game too. Rabbie Rabbit is so excited. He knows everyone will love the game of baseball.

After Rabbie explains the rules of the game and that each one will have to wear a glove on their paw, everyone is excited. Everyone except Simon.

Simon does not have a paw.
Snakes do not have paws.

Bobby Bobcat says,
"Simon, I guess you can't play with us in this game."

Simon has never been left out of any of the games they play, but he knows he cannot play baseball.

Simon is so sad. He feels so alone and begins to cry. At that very moment, Simon feels he is so different than his friends.

All his friends have paws, but he does not.

Rabbie Rabbit sees his tears.

Just then, Rabbie Rabbit has an idea. Rabbie tells Simon the game of baseball needs someone to be the umpire.

"The umpire does not have to wear a glove!" says Rabbie.
"Just pose behind home plate and call the strikes and the balls."

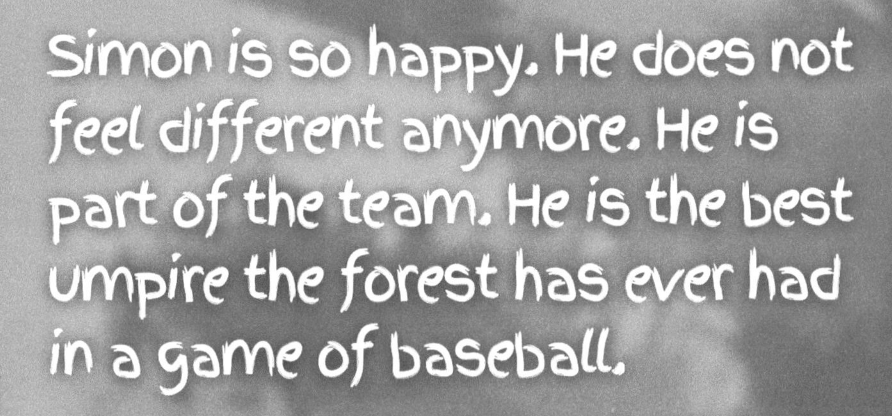

Simon is so happy. He does not feel different anymore. He is part of the team. He is the best umpire the forest has ever had in a game of baseball.

"Ssstrike three!"

calls Simon.

Simon and his friends play baseball almost every day when the sun is high in the sky and the trees are shady.

From then on, Simon knows even if he is different, he can still fit in and have friends. He just needed help from his friend Rabbie Rabbit to show him how he could contribute. Rabbie Rabbit says, "We all have a part to play, you see. Being ourselves is the best way to play."

The name of the team is Forest Friends Ball Team where everyone belongs. Simon the Snake says, "And that means you. You belong too. Welcome to the team."

Hello, boys and girls.
I hope you enjoyed reading my book. Always remember that you are very special, and no one is like you. Always try and be friendly like Simon. Good friends are good to have. Always be kind. When a friend is sad you can make that person feel better just by playing with them and being their friend.

Your friend,

Mrs. Diane

# About the Author

After reading millions of books to four-year-olds, Mrs. Diane Blue Brooks Britt finally put her own words on paper. She's a retired Pre-K teacher. One of thirteen children, Diane was raised on a farm in Robeson County. She loved telling bedtime stories to her grandchildren, Annabelle and Henry. Now, she's happy you've met Simon the Snake and his friends.

# About the Illustrator

Alyssa Grizenko is a digital illustrator specializing in character design and imaginative composition. Her stylized approach emphasizes recognizable characterization and subtle detail as distinguishing marks of her work. Alyssa loves bringing characters to life through her illustrations and enjoys partnering with writers in their projects.

In her free-time, Alyssa pursues many hobbies and interests including reading, writing, team sports, and nature walks, but her favorite activities involve participating in her local church community and spending time with her family.

Find more works by Alyssa at alyssagrizenko.com.

# Discussion Questions

1. What is your favorite game to play?
2. Have you ever invited a friend to play a game with you?
3. When you meet someone new, what can you do?
4. How can you include others around you?
5. What makes a good friend?
6. What are ways you can show you are kind?
7. What new game can you create?

# Create a New Forest Friends Game

It's fun to play new games. What new game will Simon the Snake, Rabbie Rabbit, and the forest friends play next? Please create a new game for them to play. They need your help. Draw a picture of the forest friends playing a new game. Email your illustration to Mrs. Diane. She's looking forward to hearing from you.

dianebluebrooks@gmail.com

Check out our Free Reader's Guide for Simon the Snake.

www.monarcheducationalservices.com

Printed in the USA
CPSIA information can be obtained
at www.ICGtesting.com
LVHW061205260124
769983LV00012B/44